Staying safe on the Farm with Jaxon

By Mary Boomsma
Co-authors Jaiden, Callie, and Carter Boomsma

WestBow Press books may be ordered through booksellers or by contacting:

WestBow Press
A Division of Thomas Nelson & Zondervan
1663 Liberty Drive
Bloomington, IN 47403
www.westbowpress.com
844-714-3454

Scripture quotations are taken from The Holy Bible, New International Version®, NIV® Copyright © 1973, 1978, 1984, 2011 by Biblica, Inc.® Used by permission. All rights reserved worldwide.

ISBN: 978-1-6642-4844-1 (sc)
ISBN: 978-1-6642-4845-8 (e)

Library of Congress Control Number: 2021922126

Print information available on the last page.

WestBow Press rev. date: 11/18/2021

WESTBOW
P R E S S®
A DIVISION OF THOMAS NELSON
& ZONDERVAN

Dedication Page

To our little brother,

We cannot thank you enough for every day you spent with us down here. You never failed to make us smile and brought so much happiness into our lives. We will never forget the memories you made with us. We love you so much Jax.

Love,
Jaiden, Callie, and Carter.

To our Son,

To our sweet little man, who we loved so much. You were a Mama's boy, who loved to give hugs and always made us smile. You were Dad's little hunting buddy, who loved the outdoors and being on the farm. Our hearts were broken the day you left but you will forever be in our hearts. We will see you again someday.

For God so loved the world, that he gave his only begotten Son, that whosoever believeth on him should not perish, but have eternal life. John 3:16

We Love and Miss you dearly!
Mom and Dad

Memory Page

This book was made in honor of Jaxon Liam Boomsma. In 2017, Jaxon was tragically killed in a farming accident when he was just seven years old. He loved nothing more than being on the farm. His bubbly personality and toothless smile will never be forgotten. To honor Jaxon, our family and the JLB Mission 23 Committee set up a memorial fund called the Jaxon Boomsma Memorial Fund. The JLB Mission 23 Committee was formed to help keep Jaxon's smile alive, and consists of family and friends in the Yankton community. The Jaxon Boomsma Memorial Fund has helped enhance community parks and farm safety programs. We have also set up an annual scholarship for a Yankton High School senior who will study in an agricultural related field. Our main goal is to promote farm safety and keep kids safe. As a family we wanted to be able to keep Jaxon's smile alive by helping make the places he loved safer and more beautiful for other kids. We also want to prevent more accidents from taking young lives too soon. To help donate or follow our journey, you can follow our Facebook page https://www.facebook.com/jaxonboomsma23/

Your generous giving in Jaxon's name has and will
"Keep his Smile Alive". Thank you all for the continuous support!
The Boomsma Family

There are so many fun things to do on the farm, but the most important thing is to stay safe! So, come with my grandma and I, and we'll show you how to stay safe on the farm! Whenever you are on the farm, make sure you have an adult with you. I like to help my grandpa! Kids like us need to be supervised on the farm so accidents don't happen. If you are anything like me, then you love adventure and love everything about the farm. Let's go explore the farm now!

Look over there! My grandpa is driving a tractor this way! I love the green tractors, but remember, tractors are really big and sometimes the farmer can't see what is around him. It's very important that we stay away from tractors and know where they are at all times! This tractor has a cab and a child seat. If the tractor has those two things, it's safe to ride! When grandpa's done working, maybe grandma can ask him if we can have a ride around the farm!

I love all the big machinery on the farm, especially the tractors, loaders, and combines! They are all so much fun and each have a purpose on the farm. My favorite piece of machinery is my grandpa's red semi because he uses it to transport cattle and grain. Let's go check them out!

It's important that we keep our distance when these machines are in use. They are so big that people might not see you if you are near them, and that wouldn't be good! Today they are parked, and grandma is with us, so we can get a little bit closer to them. Don't climb all over them because you might get hurt if you fall off!

You will see a lot of animals on the farm like cows, pigs, goats, horses, dogs, cats, and many more. Not all animals are pets, so make sure you know which ones you can play with before you approach them. My favorite are the kitties! Let's see if we can find my kitten, Little Ninja!

Look at all these cows! They sure are curious to see who we are. Look at them come close to the fence to see us! Grandma says the fence is secure, but we better not stand too close to it because you never know if the cows will kick the fence. Let's stay back and watch them from a distance….Mooooo! When you're around cows or horses, make sure you don't stand behind them because you might get kicked. Make sure you are very quiet and careful around animals; you don't want to spook them!

Sometimes a farmer will use an electric fence or barbed wire to keep the animals in. Electrical fences carry dangerous electric currents, so never touch that fence, and if you do, you could get shocked!

What is Uncle John doing over there by the grain bins? It looks like he is putting the grain in the feed wagon for the cows. It must be dinner time for the cattle! There is a lot of grain in the bins. Look how tall they are!

You can see there is a ladder that takes you to the top of the grain bins. I bet it would be fun to climb, but kids aren't allowed to go up there because it's way too high up! It almost touches the clouds! You also never want to go inside of the grain bins. They are very deep, and it wouldn't be good if you fell in!

Look over there! It's the shop where things get fixed! There are a lot of tools and heavy objects in there. We can peek in, but we don't want to go in there unsupervised. The farm takes a lot of work to keep running. Some of the things grandpa uses to keep the farm running are certain chemicals and gasoline. Make sure you don't get too close to those things because they are very dangerous and can make you really sick!

One of my favorite things to do on the farm is to ride the ranger and four wheelers! Be sure you don't start these by yourself, wear a helmet when you are on the four wheeler and make sure you always have an adult with you. When you go for a ride, make sure you aren't going too fast! The four wheelers are really fun when you're safe!

There are a lot of different bodies of water that could be on the farm like rivers, ponds, and dugouts, so if you are around these, make sure you're supervised. Don't get too close, we don't want anyone to fall in! Let's go look at the hay bales now!

Climbing hay bales and trees can be a lot of fun. It's best to stay off them though because you could fall and break your arm or get trapped in between the hay stacks. Remember, you can't fly, so be extremely careful climbing things such as trees, haystacks, and ladders. Only play where it's safe. We're going to go find my dad now!

I love to help my dad mow the lawn with my toy mower. I think mowing would be fun, especially with the big, riding lawn mower! Mowers can spit rocks and the blades are really sharp. I saw a rock break a window once! Just like the big machinery, you want to stay away from the mower when it's being used.

Let's go explore some more of the farm!

Yay! It's starting to get dark! Tonight we are going to roast s'mores by the fire pit! I love s'mores. I really like to make s'mores with my family. Even though it's fun, it can be dangerous too. You don't want to get burned by the flames, so you have to be careful when the fire is burning!

Farm Safety Quiz!

Here are a few questions to review your knowledge of farm safety after reading!

1. What types of clothing should you wear on the farm?
   a. Jeans and boots
   b. Pajamas
   c. A dress

2. What materials can be found in the shop?
   a. Gasoline
   b. Chemicals
   c. Tools
   d. All the above

3. True or False - You might get shocked if you touch an electrical fence.

4. True or False - You should stand behind a cow or horse to be safe.

5. True or False - Grain bins are very deep, and kids should not climb in them.

6. What two things should a tractor have for it to be safe to ride?

7. You should be _____ and _____ around animals so you don't scare them.

8. Talk to your family and see what other tips you can come up with to stay safe on the farm!

Printed in the United States
by Baker & Taylor Publisher Services